FLOODS, FLASH FLOODS, AND MUDSLIDES
A PRACTICAL SURVIVAL GUIDE

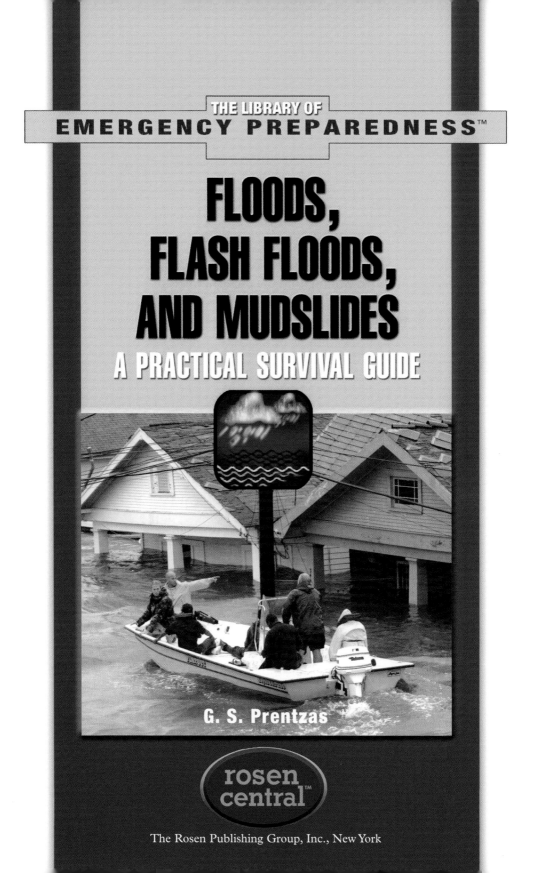

G. S. Prentzas

rosen
central™

The Rosen Publishing Group, Inc., New York

To Aunt Doris

Published in 2006 by The Rosen Publishing Group, Inc.
29 East 21st Street, New York, NY 10010

Library of Congress Cataloging-in-Publication Data

Prentzas, G. S.
Floods, flash floods, and mudslides: a practical survival guide/
G. S. Prentzas.—1st ed.
    p. cm.—(The library of emergency preparedness)
Includes bibliographical references and index.
ISBN 1-4042-0534-9 (lib. bdg.)
1. Floods. 2. Mudslides. 3. Emergency management—United States.
I. Title. II. Series.

HV609.P73 2006
363.34'93—dc22

                                                    2005016391

Manufactured in Malaysia

On the cover: Emergency workers rescue residents of Saint Bernard Parish after Hurricane Katrina hit New Orleans, Louisiana, on August 29, 2005, and caused catastrophic flooding in one of the most devastating natural disasters in U.S. history. The mayor of New Orleans had called for a mandatory evacuation of the city, but many residents refused to leave their homes.

CONTENTS

Introduction

In April 1997, heavy spring rains, combined with melting snow piled up from a series of blizzards, caused North Dakota's Red River to overflow. Grand Forks was the town hit hardest by the flood. On the *PBS NewsHour* Web site for students, an eighth-grader named Sara recounted her feelings as the flood threatened her hometown: "You couldn't flip a channel on TV without seeing the news of the flood. I was sad. Even though the river was a long way from our place, I still felt for the people who had to watch their homes go under the fearful Red River. I went to bed that night with a dread[ful] feeling in my stomach.

"By the time I went to bed, a two-foot [0.6-meter] dike covered the front of our apartment building. I was afraid to sleep. I thought that when I woke up, water would be swirling over the floor. My packed bags lay in the corner."

As the waters of the Red River rose, local officials called for a voluntary evacuation. Sara recalled, "The next morning my mom woke my sister and I up and told us to pack our things. The water was still sort of far away, but she didn't want to take any chances.

"My dad brought us to Red River High School where we took a bus to the Air Force base. My dad stayed behind to work at the hospital because there was a shortage of workers. The place we stayed in was called a hangar. It was noisy

In April 1997, the Red River encircles a section of Grand Forks, North Dakota, which remains under water. Although many of the residents had tried to use dikes and sandbags to protect their town, the citizens had to be evacuated. Once the waters receded, they were allowed to return to begin the staggering cleanup work.

and crowded. My sister had found a friend so I didn't see much of her. I was bored enough to sleep.

"The next day my dad came, and we all piled in the car and drove to my grandparents' farm in South Dakota . . . I found out that the flood waters never even entered our home. We were all thankful for that."

Despite the efforts of Grand Forks citizens, who surrounded their town with dikes constructed of sandbags, rising water poured over the dikes, flooding much of the town. The floodwaters caused catastrophic damage, estimated at more than $600 million. Sara recalled how the flood affected Grand Forks, "The town was damaged to the tiniest detail. Then we saw people cleaning and working hard. The cleaning continued and life went on, but we will always remember the Red River that devastated our city."

A flood such as the one that inundated Grand Forks, North Dakota, is not an isolated event. Floods and flash floods occur in all fifty states. Communities particularly at risk are those located in low-lying areas, near water, or downstream from a dam. Floods are dangerous, killing about 100 people each year in the United States and many more worldwide. Many people fail to realize the power of water: 6 inches (15 centimeters) of fast-moving water can knock you off your feet, and 24 inches (61 cm) of water can sweep away a car. Because of the hazards posed by floods and flash floods, it is important to find out about the potential for flooding where you live, take steps to reduce the risk for you and your family, and make flood emergency plans before a flood threatens your community.

1 --- **What Is a Flood?**

According to the World Meteorological Organization, floods are the most common and widespread of all natural disasters, except for fires. In terms of lives lost and property damaged, however, floods are the most destructive natural disaster in the United States and the world. Most U.S. communities have experienced some kind of flooding, usually after spring rains, heavy thunderstorms, or winter snow melt. Because floods can occur in any part of the country, at any time of the day, and at any time of the year, everyone needs to be aware of their dangers and prepare for them.

In general, a flood occurs when a body of water overflows and covers land that is normally dry. The National Flood Insurance Program, a U.S. government project that guarantees insurance to people who live in areas prone to floods, provides a more detailed description. It defines a flood as "a general and temporary condition of partial or complete inundation of two or more acres [0.25 hectares or more] of normally dry land . . . from the overflow of inland or tidal waters, unusual and rapid accumulation of surface waters from any source, or a mudflow."

Floods

People have chosen to live near water for thousands of years. They have planted crops in the fertile soil near rivers, and fished waterways to provide food for their families. They have used waterways as important routes of transportation and trade and to power factories.

Living near water, however, has exposed communities to the dangers of floods. For centuries, floodwaters have killed people, destroyed crops and livestock, and washed away homes, businesses, and even entire towns. Although technology and modern communications have reduced the number of deaths, floods continue to cause widespread human suffering and significant property damage.

Floods usually develop over a period of days. They do not happen simply because it rains. Floods can occur when

A "road closed" sign is mostly covered by water and chunks of ice from the Winooski River in Vermont in December 2003. Melting snow and rain showers caused the river to flood. Floods can occur when warm rain falls on snow to melt it so that the ground becomes so saturated that it cannot absorb all the water.

rain falls on ground that is already saturated, or wet. Floods can happen when warm rain falls on snow accumulations, causing the snowpack to melt rapidly. They can also occur when rain falls heavily throughout an entire valley. Floods can happen in connection with tropical storms known as hurricanes. They can also be caused by unusual events, such as dam breaks, landslides, and ice jams.

Weather cycles often cause seasonal flooding. In the United States, the combination of melting snow and rain often causes flooding in Western and Midwestern states

The Biggest Flood on Record

In the late Pleistocene era, about 15,000 years ago, ice sheets known as glaciers covered much of the area stretching from what is now Alaska south to the state of Washington and east to Montana. One of these ice sheets crept southward into the present-day Idaho panhandle, forming a large ice dam that blocked the mouth of the Clark Fork River. The ice dam created Lake Missoula, which stretched for 200 miles (322 kilometers). The ice dam eventually broke, triggering a flood that thundered downhill toward the Pacific Ocean. Moving at more than 60 miles per hour (97 km per hour), the surge of water ripped up soil and cut deep gorges into the bedrock.

Ice dams continued to re-create Lake Missoula and break, causing a flooding sequence that was repeated dozens of times. Today, the impact of these floods is easy to see. Two-hundred-ton (181-metric-ton) boulders are scattered from the Rockies to the Willamette Valley in Washington. These floodwaters also created the Grand Coulee, Dry, and Palouse waterfalls.

in the spring. Along the East Coast of the United States, heavy rains from hurricanes can cause flooding during the hurricane season, which is generally between June and November. Other countries experience floods each year during the monsoon, or rainy season. ("Monsoon" is from the Arabic word meaning "season.") An irregular weather pattern known as El Niño can lead to increased rainfall—and floods—in California and the southeastern United States.

Flash Floods

When large rivers that run through flat terrain overflow their banks, they usually do so gradually. The slowly rising water provides warning to communities that a flood is developing. An intense rainstorm, however, may over-whelm smaller rivers and streams, especially those carrying water a short distance or down steep slopes. The sudden increase in the volume of water flowing into these smaller waterways can cause dangerous overflows known as flash floods. In dry regions, heavy downpours can suddenly fill dry streambeds, known as washes, with torrents of water.

Flash floods usually occur when storms drop large amounts of rain within a brief period. They can occur with little or no warning, sometimes reaching their peak in only a few minutes. Waters move very fast during flash floods. The force can roll boulders, uproot trees, destroy buildings, and wash out bridges. Walls of water can reach as high as 10 feet (3 m) to 20 feet (6 m), carrying debris that can kill people and destroy property.

Mudslides and Landslides

Two geological hazards associated with floods are mudslides and landslides. Mudslides, also known as mudflows or debris flows, are rivers of rock, soil, and other debris saturated with water. Mudslides usually develop when water rapidly accumulates in the ground, such as during heavy rainfall or rapid snowmelt. The water changes the soil into a flowing river of mud,

Torrential rains washed out this bridge and caused a flash flood. Flash floods occur with little or no warning.

known as a slurry. Slurries can flow quickly down slopes or through channels, and they often strike with little or no warning. Slurries sometimes move at high speeds and can travel several miles from their source, growing in size as they pick up trees, cars, and other objects along the way. For example, a mudslide in La Conchita, California, on January 11, 2005, destroyed fifteen homes and killed ten residents.

Mudslides are most destructive when they are caused by volcanic eruptions. The 1980 eruption of Mount Saint Helens in Washington State, for example, melted the snow on the mountain, resulting in mudslides that destroyed bridges, roads, railways, and homes. Mudslides can also be

In La Conchita, California, a large mudslide killed ten residents and destroyed fifteen homes in January 2005. Five years earlier the city had been hit by a mudslide. The townspeople chose to reside there despite the risks of living atop hills and on slopes.

caused by severe wildfires. In July 1994, a serious wildfire in the Storm King Mountain area of Colorado stripped the slopes of vegetation, and when September rains came, mudslides blocked Interstate 70 highway and threatened to dam the Colorado River.

Landslides occur when rocks, soil, and other objects tumble down a slope. Gravity is the major force that causes landslides. Other factors—including saturation of the ground by water, earthquakes, volcanoes, and the steepening of slopes by erosion or construction—help gravity to over-come the natural resistance of the soil, leading to a landslide. Some landslides move slowly and gradually cause damage. Others move so fast that they can destroy property and take lives suddenly and unexpectedly. Landslides are usually isolated events, occurring without public warning. Generally, however, where landslides have once occurred it is likely that they will happen there again. Landslides often occur during periods of heavy rainfall or rapid snowmelt. Landslides sometimes make floods worse by clogging streams or blocking runoff with sand, mud, boulders, trees, and other materials. Each year in the United States, landslides cause as many as fifty deaths and as much as $2 billion in damages. The economic impact includes decreased property value, lost water supplies, and damage to forests, sewage systems, and roadways.

A canine search–and–rescue team checks home debris for survivors trapped inside collapsed homes after the January 2005 mudslide hit La Conchita, California. Some people believe that overdevelopment of the hillsides and excessive rainfall caused the mudslide.

Floods in the Twenty-first Century

Each year, floods kill thousands of people worldwide and cost the world economy what amounts to billions of dollars in damages. United Nations researchers have warned that the number of people exposed to the dangers of floods is expected to double to 2 billion worldwide by 2050. These researchers point to several factors that will increase the risk of floods: global warming (an increase in Earth's average temperature, which in turn causes changes in climate, including rainfall), the loss of the world's forests, rising sea levels, and population growth in flood-prone areas.

According to a June 2004 Reuters news report, Dr. Janos J. Bogardi, director of the United Nations University Institute for Environmental and Human Security, has predicted, "The world will be warmer and wetter by mid-century, and the northern part of the Northern Hemisphere will likely see more storms." Melting glaciers could make sea levels rise, leading to high water levels that will overflow small islands and cause more frequent and extreme flooding in coastal lowlands. "Most urgently needed to adapt to the growing risk of flood disasters is greater global capacity to monitor and forecast extreme events," Bogardi said. "Armed with better information [and] superior early warning systems, infrastructure can be installed and new planning strategies devised."

2 --- Where Do Floods Happen?

Although floods can strike almost anywhere, they are more likely to occur close to waterways. Areas located near a river, stream, ocean, lake, or other bodies of water are known as floodplains if they have been flooded by water in the past or could be flooded by water in the future. Rivers with large floodplains include the Mississippi River (in the United States), the Nile (in northeast Africa), the Ganges (in India), and the Huang He River (in China; also known as the Yellow River). The size of a specific floodplain depends on many factors, including the height, or elevation, of the land; the size and volume, or flow, of the waterway; and the amount of territory drained by the waterway.

Hydrologists, or scientists who study the distribution of water, rate the severity of floods in a floodplain by predicting the likelihood that they will occur in a certain amount of time. The limit of a specific area that is flooded an average of once a year is known as the one-year flood level. One-year floods usually cause little damage because people expect them to happen and avoid building houses or planting crops on the land. A ten-year flood level means that there's a one in ten chance each year that floodwaters will cover certain lands next to a river. (A ten-year flood will overflow land farther away from the river, or at higher elevation, than the land covered by a one-year flood.)

This map depicts the Mississippi River basin of the United States. The basin is particularly vulnerable to floods and droughts. Extremes in weather, such as the El Niño weather cycle, can worsen the dangerous effects of weather in the basin area.

Hydrologists determine flood frequencies by plotting a graph of the size of all known floods for an area and determining how often floods of a particular size occur.

Scientists and government officials often use the term "100-year flood" to describe a rare, large-scale flood that occurs once in 100 years on average. This does not mean that a 100-year flood will occur once every 100 years. A 100-year flood might occur more than once in a century, or it may not occur at all during that time. In many locations, changing weather patterns, an increase in urban development, and the cutting down of forests have reduced the land's natural ability to absorb water. These factors have made floods more likely to occur now and in the future than past flood events would indicate.

Major Storms and Seasonal Rains

Storms producing heavy rains are the leading cause of floods. These storms can strike at any time of the year, but in the United States, they usually occur in spring and summer. Spring flooding is common in the northern and western regions of the country. At the beginning of spring, all the snow that has accumulated over the winter, known as the snowpack, begins to melt. If heavy rains occur during this time, rivers will overflow their banks because they cannot handle all that water at once. In summer, thunderstorms are common throughout the country and can cause flooding anywhere.

☁ The Dartmouth Flood Observatory ☁

The Dartmouth Flood Observatory is a research project supported by the National Aeronautics and Space Administration (NASA) and Dartmouth University. The observatory, located in Lebanon, New Hampshire, uses satellite images to detect, map, measure, and analyze extreme flood events on rivers worldwide. The observatory also provides yearly catalogs, large-scale maps, and images of river floods, dating from 1985 to the present. The observatory aims to collect enough reliable information to help flood forecasters improve their predictions about when and where major flooding will occur.

A satellite of the National Oceanic and Atmospheric Administration (NOAA), a scientific agency responsible for weather forecasting and ocean charting and research, took this image showing the eye of a tropical storm moving along the southeastern coast of South Carolina in August 2004. The NOAA issued a flash flood watch for the area.

In other parts of the world, extreme seasonal rains known as monsoons produce floods at particular seasons each year. In India, the rainy season lasts from June through September. In Southeast Asia and in the Southern Hemisphere, monsoon rains pour from November to April. Heavy monsoon rains can devastate vast areas. In India, for example, the waters of the Ganges River system, which includes the Brahmaputra and Meghna rivers, can swell dramatically during the monsoon season, affecting the lives of hundreds of thousands of people living along the river. In July 2005, 37 inches (94 cm) of rain fell in Mumbai, India, in twenty-four hours. Water levels rose more than 7 feet (2.1 m) in some places, and more than a thousand people in the region were killed.

In the United States, during El Niño years (which have occurred on average twenty times each century), California and the southeastern United States usually receive higher than average rainfall. El Niño arises when waters in the central Pacific Ocean become unusually warm. El Niño's sister phenomenon, La Niña, occurs when these waters become unusually cool. Both El Niño and La Niña lead to disruptions in weather and climate around the world. El Niño sometimes triggers heavy rains that create floods. In January 1997, El Niño storms caused the Russian River and other waterways in northern California to flood, resulting in more than $2 billion in damage.

Dam Breaks

Dams are natural or human-made barriers that prevent water from flowing. Areas lying downstream from dams are at risk of floods because dams sometimes break. Although most dams, including such well-known structures as the Grand Coulee and Hoover dams, are amazing feats of engineering and construction, others are not built as well. Dams usually break because

People who survived the Johnstown, Pennsylvania, flood in May 1889 stand beside homes that were destroyed when the South Fork Dam collapsed.

of poor design, age, or inadequate maintenance. Sometimes dams break when they suffer structural damage during earthquakes. Dam failures are potentially the worst flood events, suddenly releasing enormous amounts of water. These waters race downstream, often destroying everything in their path.

Hurricanes and Tsunamis

Areas near oceans are also susceptible to flooding during severe tropical storms known as hurricanes. A hurricane has sustained winds of at least 73.6 miles per hour (118.5 km/h). Although hurricane winds are dangerous, water usually causes the most damage. Hurricane winds push coastal tides

In Banda Aceh, Indonesia, a resident returns to an area that was demolished by a tsunami on December 26, 2004. An earthquake in the Indian Ocean near the island of Sumatra triggered the tsunami, a series of giant waves propelled shoreward.

much higher than normal, sending seawater crashing over coastal lowlands. This wall of water is known as a storm surge. As hurricanes move inland, they lessen in intensity but can produce heavy rains. These downpours can cause floods and flash floods. In August 2005, heavy rains and high winds associated with Hurricane Katrina caused major flooding from Fort Lauderdale, Florida, where it made its first landfall, to near New Orleans, Louisiana, where it made another landfall after regaining strength in the warm waters of the Gulf of Mexico. Hurricane Katrina hit the Louisiana-Mississippi border with 140-mph (225 km/h) winds and a storm surge almost 30 feet (9 m) high. About 80 percent of New Orleans was flooded, with some areas under 20 feet (6 m) of water. Sections of three levees collapsed, sending water from Lake Pontchartrain streaming into the city. Despite being downgraded to a tropical depression, Katrina's winds continued farther inland, through the Ohio Valley and eastern Great Lakes area. Tornadoes and flooding were reported along the storm's path.

Another coastal phenomenon related to floods is the tsunami. Named after the Japanese word for "harbor wave," tsunamis are triggered by shockwaves from earthquakes or by landslides that occur beneath the ocean floor. These waves travel unnoticed across an entire ocean, eventually piling water up against an unsuspecting coastline far away. Tsunamis can be extremely destructive. On December 26, 2004, an exceptionally strong earthquake produced a tsunami wave that reached 100 feet (30 m) in height. The wave caused widespread damage and killed more than 300,000 people in Indonesia, Thailand, Sri Lanka, and other countries.

3 --- Flood Preparedness

Communities threatened by flooding can take steps to reduce the chances of floods and to lessen the damage that they cause. Many communities located in areas prone to flooding can develop floodplain management plans. They can also build flood barriers to control water over-flows. Homeowners and businesses can reduce the potential financial impact of flood damage by buying flood insurance. People living in floodplains can prepare for a flood emergency by developing a personal flood emergency plan and putting together a supply kit in case evacuation becomes necessary.

Floodplain Management

With assistance from federal and state governments, most cities and counties in flood zones have developed methods to manage waters and lowlands. Many have passed laws that prohibit or restrict construction in the areas most at-risk for flooding. Zoning ordinances, building codes, and other regulations control the construction of houses and businesses in floodplains. The steady demand for additional housing, businesses, and industrial facilities, however, means that new construction still occurs in floodplains throughout the United States.

Floodplain management has three major goals. It seeks to lower the risk of flood losses through laws, flood forecasting, emergency preparedness, and flood proofing. It tries to reduce potential flood damage by building flood barriers and using such flood control techniques as dredging river channels (which improves the flow of water downstream), diverting high water into undeveloped lowlands, and shoreline protection (such as planting vegetation to stop riverbank erosion). Finally, it seeks to lessen the impact of floods through education, flood insurance, disaster assistance, and post-flood recovery programs. The management of floodplains requires striking a delicate balance between improving community safety and maintaining economic opportunities for residents.

Flood Barriers

Flood barriers can provide communities with some protection from floodwaters. Dams, levees, and floodwalls are the most popular types of flood control structures. A dam is a wall built across a stream or river to hold back the water. Usually constructed of reinforced concrete, dams can be used to prevent floods, generate electricity, and provide drinking water and recreational facilities. In the United States, there are nearly 100,000 dams. Levees and dikes are walls built alongside rivers to prevent water from overflowing riverbanks. They are usually made of earth and are often the barriers that break or overflow during extreme flooding. Floodwalls are concrete walls that act as barriers against floodwaters. They are usually built in areas with a limited amount of space.

Dams, levees and dikes, floodwalls, and other flood control projects provide protection against a certain level of flooding. The level of protection is often based on the potential for damage, environmental impact, and cost.

🌩 U.S. Army Corps of Engineers 🌩

The United States Army Corps of Engineers (USACE) is a division of the U.S. Army that provides engineering services to the armed forces and to the nation. The USACE employs engineers, scientists, and other specialists focused on public engineering and environmental matters. Its staff is mostly civilian personnel (numbering about 35,000) rather than military personnel (about 700). The Flood Control Act of 1936 gave responsibility for most federal flood control projects to the USACE. Since then, corps engineers, hydrologists, geologists, biologists, and natural resource managers have worked on a wide range of flood control projects, particularly along the Mississippi River.

The USACE has built and maintained dams and reservoirs, which hold excess water upstream. When storms hit, USACE employees gradually release the water from the dams to prevent or reduce downstream flooding. The corps has also built and maintained other flood control structures—such as levees, floodwalls, and diversion channels—to protect cities near waterways. These flood control barriers keep water out of homes, schools, and businesses in cities near waterways. The USACE also helps reduce flood damage by preventing additional construction in areas most prone to floods. Along coastlines, the corps erects barriers, builds breakwaters, and reinforces dunes and beaches to reduce coastal flooding and erosion.

Students toured the Hartwell Dam and lake, which is located in the Savannah River basin in Georgia, near Hartwell, in 2002. The U.S. Army Corps of Engineers designed and built the dam for flood control and to help supply water to residents living downstream. The Hartwell Dam is unique for its exterior power plant, which provides hydroelectricity.

Major flood control projects in the United States are located along the Colorado River (including the Hoover Dam), the Columbia River (including the Grand Coulee Dam), the Mississippi River, and the Tennessee River. The Mississippi River has a long history of devastating floods, and many attempts have been made to control its waters. For the past seventy years, the U.S. Army Corps of Engineers has built many levees, dams, and diversions along the Mississippi River.

Because flood control projects alter the flow of water, they can have a major impact on a river—locally, upstream, and downstream. Federal, state, and local governments often act together to ensure that flood control projects do not transfer flood risks from one community to another.

Other Measures

In addition to passing zoning laws and building flood barriers, communities can take other measures to reduce the risk of floods and the damages that they cause. Local governments can buy properties in the most vulnerable part of the floodplain and turn them into greenways, parks, or other venues that will suffer minimal damage from floodwaters. They can develop and improve flood preparedness plans and warning systems to alert residents of imminent flooding. They can educate residents about flood dangers and provide technical and financial assistance to property owners in protecting their property against flooding.

Flood Insurance

The risk of experiencing a flood depends on where you live. There are many different flood zones throughout the United States, and each has a different level of risk. You can view the level of flood risk to your community at the Web site of the Federal Emergency Management Agency (FEMA) listed in the For More Information section at the back of this book. Families that live in areas prone to flooding can buy flood insurance to cover losses resulting from flood damage. Insurance for landslides is generally not available, but in some cases flood insurance policies will cover mudslide damage.

Flood insurance will pay the cost of rebuilding, but it needs to be purchased before a flood occurs. It usually takes thirty days after purchase for the insurance policy to go into effect. Anyone can buy flood insurance as long as the property is located in a community that participates in the

National Flood Insurance Program. Homes, condominiums, apartments, and business structures are all eligible. Residents can buy flood insurance even if the property has been flooded before. Renters may also purchase flood insurance for their possessions. FEMA oversees flood insurance through its National Flood Insurance Program. The U.S. government sets the prices for flood insurance, so the rate is the same from all insurance companies that offer it. Keep in mind that standard homeowners' insurance policies do not cover flood damage, so buying a separate flood insurance policy is necessary. Once you have flood insurance, make a list of all your important possessions (including model and serial numbers) and take photos or videos of them and store the documents in another location. These documents will help you if you have to file a flood insurance claim.

Flood Preparedness

In addition to buying flood insurance, you and your family can take other actions before a flood occurs to ensure safety and to reduce any financial losses that may result. The first step is to gather information about the flood hazard in your community. Contact your local emergency management or civil defense office, National Weather Service office, or American Red Cross chapter. Ask about the history of flooding in your neighborhood and whether your family's property is above or below flooding level. Learn about your community's warning system, evacuation plans, and emergency shelter locations.

You and your family should prepare an emergency plan for everyone to follow in the event of a potential flood. Post

Members of the National Guard and high school students rushed with sandbags to reinforce a dike in St. Paul, Minnesota. The Mississippi River runs through St. Paul and Minneapolis, Minnesota, and often overflows its banks. Always ask about the history of flooding in your community and whether your family's home is above or below the flooding level.

emergency phone numbers by the telephone. Everyone in the household should know to dial 911 (or your local emergency number) in case of emergency. Plan and practice a flood evacuation route with your family. Make sure to identify alternate routes in case the main route is blocked by water or jammed with traffic.

Your family could be anywhere when a flood strikes—at work, at school, or in the car. Make sure that you know how to reach each other. Ask an out-of-state relative or friend to be the family contact in case your family is separated during a flood. Make sure everyone knows the name, address, and phone number of this contact person. Know the directions to emergency shelters in your area and identify alternates in case flooding closes these shelters. Many shelters do not allow pets (except for service animals, such as dog guides, assisting people who are blind), so make a pet evacuation plan. Your local animal shelter, veterinarian, or local humane society can provide you with information and guidance. The Humane Society of the United States recommends that you never leave pets behind in an emergency. Many hotels or motels will accept pets in an emergency. Also remember to keep up-to-date

Teenagers played basketball at the Red Cross shelter in Trenton, New Jersey, after rivers in central and northern New Jersey flooded during heavy rains in April 2005. You and your family should prepare an emergency plan, which includes knowing which disaster shelter is nearest to your home.

identification tags on your pets and have on hand a pet survival kit with your pets' medical records, medications, and food. Keep your pet in a kennel carrier or on a leash to ensure its safety. Because an evacuation can be sudden and disorganized, make a to-do checklist beforehand to ensure that nothing important is forgotten or left behind.

You and your family should store important documents and irreplaceable personal items (such as photographs) where they won't get damaged. If major flooding is

YOUR FLOOD EMERGENCY KIT

You and your family should also put together a flood emergency kit. At minimum, your emergency supply kit should include the following items:

✓ Water: a three-day supply; each person will need 2 gallons (7.6 liters) of water per day for drinking, washing, and other uses

✓ Food: a three-day supply (nonperishable food, such as canned meat, vegetables, fruit, and beverages)

✓ Flashlights and replacement batteries

✓ 100-hour candle (but do not use it if there is a chance of a gas leak)

✓ Emergency reflective blanket and a lightweight wool blanket (optional: sleeping bags and other camping gear)

✓ Hats and gloves

✓ Waterproof poncho

✓ Rubber boots

✓ Rubber gloves (two pairs)

✓ Extra clothing

✓ Hand and body warmers

✓ Battery-operated radio with replacement batteries (also recommended: special NOAA weather radio)

✓ Waterproof matches (held in a waterproof container) and butane lighter

✓ Pocketknife

✓ Duct tape

✓ Whistle

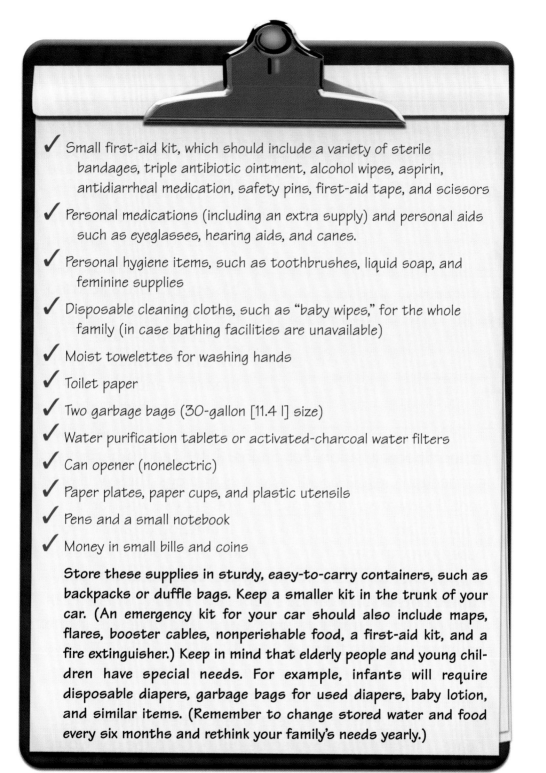

✓ Small first-aid kit, which should include a variety of sterile bandages, triple antibiotic ointment, alcohol wipes, aspirin, antidiarrheal medication, safety pins, first-aid tape, and scissors

✓ Personal medications (including an extra supply) and personal aids such as eyeglasses, hearing aids, and canes.

✓ Personal hygiene items, such as toothbrushes, liquid soap, and feminine supplies

✓ Disposable cleaning cloths, such as "baby wipes," for the whole family (in case bathing facilities are unavailable)

✓ Moist towelettes for washing hands

✓ Toilet paper

✓ Two garbage bags (30-gallon [11.4 l] size)

✓ Water purification tablets or activated-charcoal water filters

✓ Can opener (nonelectric)

✓ Paper plates, paper cups, and plastic utensils

✓ Pens and a small notebook

✓ Money in small bills and coins

Store these supplies in sturdy, easy-to-carry containers, such as backpacks or duffle bags. Keep a smaller kit in the trunk of your car. (An emergency kit for your car should also include maps, flares, booster cables, nonperishable food, a first-aid kit, and a fire extinguisher.) Keep in mind that elderly people and young children have special needs. For example, infants will require disposable diapers, garbage bags for used diapers, baby lotion, and similar items. (Remember to change stored water and food every six months and rethink your family's needs yearly.)

FLOOD PREPARATION CHECKLIST

- Gather information on the flood history of your community, including flood evacuation routes.
- Prepare a family flood emergency plan (including one for pets, if relevant).
- Store important documents in a safe, watertight place.
- Prepare your house for the flood.
- Put together a family flood emergency kit.

expected, consider putting them in a storage facility far removed from the flood zone. If you have a basement, install a sump pump with back-up power. This device will pump water out of the basement. Have a licensed electrician raise electric components—such as switches, sockets, circuit breakers, and wiring—at least 12 inches (30.5 cm) above your home's projected flood elevation. For drains, toilets, and other sewer connections, install backflow valves or plugs. These will prevent floodwaters from entering your house. Anchor or tie down oil and propane tanks. An unanchored tank in your basement can be torn free by floodwaters, and the broken supply line can contaminate your basement. An unanchored outside tank can be swept downstream, where it can damage other houses. If your washer and dryer are in the basement, elevate them at least 12 inches (30.5 cm) above the projected flood elevation. Place the furnace and water heater at least 12 inches (30.5 cm) above the projected flood elevation as well. If water were to reach the furnace or water heater, the pilot flame would be put out and the gas would continue to flow, risking an explosion and fire. Therefore, turn off the gas lines if open flames might be flooded.

4 --- Flood Warnings and Survival

Many of the deaths and injuries caused by floods are avoidable. The main reason that floods kill or injure people is that many underestimate the power of water. Many flood hazards can be avoided by becoming familiar with the dangers posed by floods, taking flood warnings seriously, and following safety recommendations.

Flood Watches and Flood Warnings

The National Weather Service (NWS) is the government agency responsible for warning the public about possible flooding. Across the country, NWS scientists watch storm activity, measure rainfall, and issue flood advisories when necessary. Using computer models that simulate river flow, snowpack depth, and rainfall, NWS regional river forecast centers make flood predictions and alert radio and television stations. The NWS also broadcasts updated weather warnings twenty-four hours a day. Special weather radios, which are sold in many stores, can receive these weather alerts. Their average range is 40 miles (64.4 km), depending on the local landscape. The NWS recommends buying a weather radio that has both a battery backup and a tone-alert feature, which automatically alerts you when a watch or warning is issued for your community.

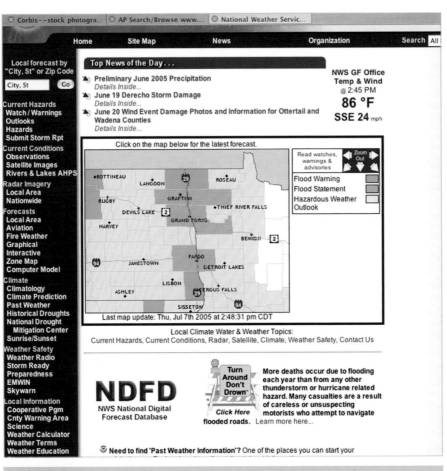

The National Weather Service (NWS) issued this map depicting a flood warning in July 2005 for the Roseau River region in northwestern Minnesota. The NWS updates weather warnings around the clock at its Web site (http://www.nws.noaa.gov).

Based on past weather records, current weather patterns, and observations of the water levels of rivers and streams, the NWS may decide to issue a flood advisory. Depending on the local conditions and likelihood of flooding, the NWS will issue one of five different warning messages: a small stream advisory, flood watch, flood warning, flash flood watch, or flash flood warning. When smaller streams begin to flood, the NWS may issue a small stream advisory. This means that minor flooding is occurring in low-lying areas. A flood watch is issued when flooding within a designated watch area is possible but not certain. People in the watch area are advised to stay tuned to the latest weather broadcasts and to be prepared to move to higher ground if a flood warning is issued. If significant flooding is already in progress or is likely to take place, the NWS will issue a flood warning. A flood warning means that flooding along larger streams

FLOOD ADVISORY CHECKLIST

Take the following actions in the event of flood advisories:

- Small stream advisory: Stay away from small streams.

- Flood watch: Tune in to the radio and television to keep informed of the latest weather conditions. Be prepared to take the appropriate action in the event a flood warning is announced for your location.

- Flood warning: Head for higher ground or evacuate, if necessary.

- Flash flood watch and warning: Evacuate low-lying areas immediately.

- There are two simple rules for remaining safe in any flooding situation: head for higher ground, and stay away from floodwaters.

has been reported or is imminent, presenting a serious threat to life or property. You should take necessary precautions at once. The NWS will issue a flash flood watch when conditions are favorable for a flash flood. They will issue a flash flood warning when a flash flood has been reported or is about to happen. Because flash floods are particularly life threatening, people should move to higher ground immediately whenever the NWS issues a flash flood watch or warning. Following a flood or flash flood, the NWS will issue a flood or flash flood statement, which provides detailed information about what occurred during the flood event.

Mudslide and Landslide Warning Signs

Check with your local building or planning department to find out whether you live in a landslide area. If your home is located in an area prone to mudslides or landslides, remain aware of conditions during heavy rainstorms. Watch the hillsides around your home for any signs of land movement, such as small landslides, debris flows, or trees starting to tilt. Many mudslide deaths occur when people are sleeping, so stay awake if you're concerned about a landslide during heavy rains. The U.S. Geological Survey provides in-depth information on landslides on its Web site, which is listed in the For More Information section at the back of this book. To prepare for a potential landslide you can use the flood emergency and evacuation checklists found in this chapter.

What to Do When a Flood Arrives

Once floodwaters are rising, nothing can stop them. By making the preparations recommended in chapter 3, you will be in better shape to face a flood that threatens your home. You can take additional steps to make sure your family remains safe until the water levels drop again. Stay tuned to the television and radio for official announcements. Listen for disaster sirens and warning signals (make sure that you are familiar with your community's warning signals). Review your emergency plans and check to see whether any items are missing from your flood emergency kit. Stay in touch

Student volunteers fill sandbags in a downpour to help protect Fowler High School in Kansas in June 2005. In some instances, the use of sandbags can prevent rising water from seeping into an area. If you live in a floodplain, have plastic or burlap bags, sand, and shovels available for flood emergencies.

with relatives. Store valuables and other important items—such as mortgage papers, medical records, birth certificates, marriage certificates, wills, bank account numbers, credit card account numbers, and insurance policies—in water-proof containers and place them on an upper level of your home. Make sure that the fuel tanks of all vehicles are full, in case they are needed for an evacuation. If no vehicle is available, make arrangements with neighbors, friends, or family for transportation.

In some cases, you may be able to protect your home from floodwaters by surrounding it with sandbags. You'll need burlap or plastic bags, sand, and shovels. The U.S.

FLOOD EMERGENCY CHECKLIST

- Stay tuned to weather reports.
- Review your emergency plan, including the best route to higher ground.
- Store valuable items in a safe place, preferably on the higher floors in your home.
- Put fuel in vehicles.
- Stockpile water.
- Shut off utilities, if necessary.

Army Corps of Engineers provides detailed information on how to use sandbags on its Web site, which is listed in the For More Information section at the back of this book.

Fill bathtubs, sinks, and containers with clean water, in the event that your local water supply becomes contaminated. Adjust the thermostat on refrigerators and freezers to the coolest possible setting so that the temperature inside will be as cold as possible, in case the power goes out. If local authorities instruct you to do so, turn off electricity at the main power switch and close the main gas valve. This will prevent electric shocks when the power is restored and gas leaks. Also close the house's main water valve. Stock up on food supplies that require little or no cooking. Move outdoor belongings, such as patio furniture, indoors. Never play around streams, rivers, storm drains, or viaducts during a flood. Fast-moving water can sweep you downstream.

Evacuation

The NWS recommends that residents leave a potential flood area early, when evacuation is still voluntary. A voluntary evacuation means that people are advised to relocate to a safer area, but they are not required to leave the anticipated flood zone. Floodwaters occasionally rise quicker or higher than expected, however, cutting off escape routes. People sometimes find themselves in dangerous situations when they fail to evacuate a flood zone promptly. If local officials announce a mandatory evacuation, that means everyone (except authorized personnel) should leave the area. People who do not comply with a mandatory evacuation order will not be arrested, but they should not count on rescue or other life-saving assistance after the onset of the flooding.

Local authorities post evacuation routes, pictured here, during flood emergencies. Always follow the designated route.

If instructed to evacuate your home, either by authorities or by an NWS flood warning for your area, do so immediately. Never ignore an evacuation order or flood warning. Move to a safe area before access is cut off by floodwater. Follow recommended escape routes. They have been selected because they are safe and provide the best means of escaping floodwaters. Keep in mind that shortcuts may go through low-lying areas and could be blocked by water. Local fire and police departments usually assist communities with evacuation. In larger evacuations, the U.S. National Guard and U.S. Coast Guard will help.

EVACUATION CHECKLIST

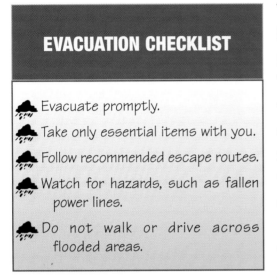

☁ Evacuate promptly.

☁ Take only essential items with you.

☁ Follow recommended escape routes.

☁ Watch for hazards, such as fallen power lines.

☁ Do not walk or drive across flooded areas.

They sometimes use boats or helicopters to rescue trapped residents. Take only essential items with you. Your flood emergency kit (see chapter 3) should contain all essential items. Follow the designated evacuation routes, but expect heavy traffic. Inform neighbors and authorities of your

A search and rescue team from San Diego, California, navigates a boat through the flood waters of New Orleans, Louisiana, in September 2005, searching for survivors after Hurricane Katrina hit the Gulf region. Because Hurricane Katrina caused massive devastation in Louisiana and Mississippi, search and rescue teams from around the country were mobilized to assist local police and fire departments and the U.S. military in searching for people who had not followed evacuation orders.

☁ Cars and Floods ☁

Most flood deaths in the United States involve automobiles. Many of these deaths are preventable. Drivers should always turn around when they encounter a flooded roadway. It is difficult to judge the depth of water, the speed of the current, or the condition of the road beneath the water. Drivers should never pull around any barrier warning that the road ahead is flooded. Drivers should be especially cautious at night, when it is harder to recognize flood hazards.

Rising waters can cause a car to stall, and fast-moving water can sweep cars downstream. If your family's car stalls, abandon it immediately and climb to higher ground. If rising water traps your car, open a door or window to let water inside so the car won't float. As little as 2 feet (0.6 m) of water will carry away most cars. Climb on to the car's roof and wait for help.

During a flood watch, a road sign next to the Concord River in Massachusetts announces that the road was flooded. If you get trapped in a car on a flooded road, abandon the car and try to climb to higher ground.

intention to leave and where you plan to go in case they need to contact you.

Evacuations save lives, but they can involve complications. Traffic often clogs escape routes. Electrical wires, water, and fallen trees can block roadways. Shelters are often overcrowded. While evacuating, never walk through flooded areas. As little as 6 inches (15 cm) of moving water can knock you off of your feet. Do not drive through a flooded area. If you come to a flooded road, turn around and go another way. Do not try to swim to safety. Wait for rescuers to come to you. Stay away from fallen power lines and electrical wires. Electrocution is a major cause of death in floods because electric current travels easily through water.

Tennessee firefighters rescue two teenagers from the roof of their car during a flood. In deep water, escape a sinking car by opening the windows immediately and swimming out. Tests have shown that you should not wait until the water has entirely filled the car. Try to escape immediately.

If you are unable to evacuate safely and rising floodwaters trap you in your house, stay in the house. If the waters start to rise inside your house, retreat to the second floor. If they continue to rise, retreat to the attic or, if necessary, the roof. Take dry clothing, a flashlight, a portable radio, and a mobile phone with you. Call or wait for help to arrive.

If you come into contact with floodwaters, wash your hands with soap and clean water as soon as possible. Floodwaters may carry raw sewage, chemical waste, and other harmful or disease-spreading substances. Look out for animals, especially snakes. Floods drive animals from their homes, and they may seek shelter in yours.

If you find yourself outdoors during a flood, climb to high ground and stay there. Evacuate canyons, washes, dips (downward inclinations), and other low-lying areas whenever a flash flood watch or warning has been issued anywhere in the area. In dry regions, runoff from thunderstorms can cause flash floods many miles away.

5 --- After the Flood

Floods, mudslides, and landslides can devastate communities by damaging roads, bridges, railroad tracks, gas and water pipelines, telephone lines, and other infrastructure. They also disrupt lives by destroying homes, businesses, and jobs. Floods can destroy crops and livestock, leading to higher food prices and, in some cases, famine.

Flood, mudslide, and landslide dangers do not end when the water begins to recede. Listen to a local radio or television station for official announcements, and do not return home until the authorities indicate that it is safe to do so. Local police and the National Guard will cordon off a flooded area until it is safe to allow residents to return to their homes and businesses. When returning to a home that's been flooded, be aware of the safety and health risks to your family.

Health and Safety Concerns

Before reentering your home, check for structural damage. Inspect the foundation for cracks or other damage. Do not go into the building if there is a chance that it will collapse. Wear sturdy, waterproof boots and be careful walking around. After a flood, steps and floors are often slippery with mud and covered with debris, including nails and broken glass. Look for electrical system damage. If you see sparks or broken or frayed wires, turn off the electricity at

Flood insurance adjusters assess the damage to a Mississippi home after a flood in 1993. Flood preparedness includes providing flood insurance for your family's home. If your house has been damaged in a flood, you must call the insurance company to file a claim. If you are unable to occupy your home, make sure that your family saves receipts for all your expenses during your stay in temporary housing.

the main fuse box or circuit breaker. Keep the power turned off until an electrician has made a safety inspection. If you have to step into water to get to the fuse box or circuit breaker, call an electrician for advice.

Special care must be taken if your home has gas appliances. Be sure to check for gas leaks. If you smell gas or hear hissing, open a window, leave quickly, and call the gas company once you have left the house. Do not use matches or any other open flame inside the house until you have confirmed that there is no gas leak. Turn off the gas at the outside main valve if you can, and call the gas company from a neighbor's home. If the gas main has been turned off, call a professional to turn it back on.

Check your water and sewage lines for damage. If you suspect damage, do not use tap water or the toilet. Call a plumber. Floods can damage water and sewer pipes. Disease-causing bacteria in sewage can enter the water supply. These bacteria can cause many serious illnesses, including diarrhea, cholera, dysentery, and typhoid fever. Until the local authorities announce that your water supply is safe, boil water vigorously for at least ten minutes before using it. Do not use contaminated water to wash dishes, brush your teeth, or prepare food. If you use bottled water, be sure that it came from a safe source. If boiling water is not possible, use water purification tablets (chlorine or iodine) and carefully follow the directions on the bottle. Treating water with chlorine or iodine tablets will kill most bacteria in the water but will not kill harmful parasites. If your water comes from a well, it will need to be tested and disinfected after floodwaters recede. Questions about testing should be directed to your local or state health department.

To prevent illness, always wash your hands with soap and water that has been boiled before preparing or eating food, after toilet use, after participating in flood cleanup activities, and after handling articles contaminated with floodwater. If you receive a puncture wound or if any wound comes into contact with floodwater, have a doctor determine whether a tetanus booster is necessary.

Do not eat any food that may have come into contact with floodwater. For infants, use only canned baby formula that requires no added water, rather than powdered formulas that have to be prepared with water. Discard any refrigerated or frozen food that has been at room temperature for two hours or longer, and any food that has an unusual odor, color, or texture. To be safe, remember, "When in doubt, throw it out."

Many wild animals, especially poisonous snakes, have been forced from their natural habitats by flooding, and many domestic animals are also without homes after a flood. Take care to avoid these animals. If an animal must be removed, contact local animal control authorities. If any animal bites you, seek immediate medical attention. Contact local or state health and agricultural officials for state guidelines on disposal of dead animals.

Be aware of potential chemical hazards you may encounter during the aftermath of a flood. Floodwaters

In Missouri, farmers tried to rescue more than 2,500 pigs during the flooding of the Mississippi River. Always use caution when handling animals during disasters. The unfamiliar situation and excitement can frighten them, and they might bite or kick in self-defense. Contact animal control authorities to help in emergency situations.

POSTFLOOD SAFETY CHECKLIST

- Check your home for structural damage. Take pictures for insurance claims.
- Wear protective clothing.
- Check sewer and water lines, electricity, and gas utilities.
- Drink bottled or boiled water.
- Wash hands with clean water.
- Throw out any food that might be contaminated.

may have buried or moved hazardous containers of solvents or other industrial chemicals from their normal storage places. Do not attempt to move propane or oil tanks. Consult your local police or fire department or emergency management agency for assistance.

Remember to help any neighbors who may require special assistance, particularly families with infants, elderly people, or people with special needs.

The weeks after a flood are difficult. In addition to keeping an eye on everyone's physical health, you and your family should remain aware of each family member's mental health. Remember that some sleeplessness, anxiety, anger, hyperactivity, mild depression, and lethargy are normal. These symptoms may go away with time. If you or any family member feels any of these symptoms acutely, however, seek some counseling. State and local health departments will help you find the necessary local resources.

Cleaning Up and Rebuilding

If floodwater has entered your family's home, it is important to dry it out as soon as possible to prevent the growth of molds. A mold is a type of fungus that grows in a damp environment. Exposure to molds can have various effects on human health, including irritation of the eyes, difficulty in breathing, and rashes. Mold can sometimes be recognized by sight (discolored walls or ceilings, signs of water damage) or smell (a musty, earthy odor). If your home has been flooded and has been closed up for several days, assume your home has been contaminated with mold, even if you cannot see or smell it. The Environmental Protection Agency (EPA) provides a guide to cleaning up mold on its Web site, which is listed in the For More Information section at the back of this book.

If an electrician has determined that it is safe to use electricity, use an electric pump or wet-dry shop vacuum to remove standing water. Pump out flooded basements gradually to avoid structural damage. Be sure to wear rubber boots. If it is unsafe to use electricity, you can use a portable generator to power pumps and vacuums. If weather permits, open windows and doors of the house to aid in the drying-out process. Use fans and dehumidifiers to remove excess moisture. Fans should be placed at a window or door to blow the air outward rather than inward to keep from spreading mold spores. Have your home heating, ventilating, and air-conditioning (HVAC) system checked and cleaned by a professional. This will kill mold and prevent later mold growth. Once the HVAC system has been cleaned, you can turn it on to help remove moisture from your house.

Walls, hard-surfaced floors, and many other household surfaces should be cleaned with soap and water and disinfected with a solution of 1 cup (237 milliliters) of bleach to

This resident of Biloxi, Mississippi, sorts through the rubble of his home after Hurricane Katrina's winds and floodwaters destroyed it in August 2005. If your home has been damaged by a flood, make sure that local authorities have given the OK before returning to it. If your family members have flood insurnace, they should immediately file a claim with their insurance agent. FEMA and the EPA provide guidelines for home cleanup after floods.

5 gallons (19 l) of water. Wash all linens and clothing in hot water or have them dry-cleaned. For items that cannot be washed or dry-cleaned, such as mattresses and upholstered furniture, air dry them in the sun and then spray them thoroughly with a disinfectant. Steam clean all carpets and rugs. Remove and discard contaminated household materials that cannot be disinfected, such as wall coverings and drywall.

When salvaging water-damaged books, heirlooms, photographs, textiles, currency, and other property, follow the restoration tips provided on FEMA's Web site, which is listed in the For More Information section of this book.

If your home has suffered damage and your family has flood insurance, call your insurance agent to file a claim. If you are unable to stay in your home, make sure to tell the agent where you can be reached. FEMA recommends that policyholders take photos of any water in the house and save damaged property to make filing a claim easier.

Disaster Relief

When a flood displaces people, they often are unsure about what to do. Where will they live? Where will they eat? How

☁ Lending a Helping Hand ☁

When a flood devastates a community, people everywhere want to help those in need. This compassion and generosity can be put to best use by following these recommendations. Flood victims have an immediate need for financial assistance. Financial contributions should be made through a recognized organization. Before donating food or clothing, you should wait for instructions from local officials. Immediately after a disaster, these items often go unused because relief workers usually do not have the time or facilities to distribute the donated goods to flood victims.

Volunteers should contact a recognized organization, such as the American Red Cross. These organizations have much experience dealing with the aftermath of floods and other disasters. They are prepared to help flood victims and are ready to accept the assistance of volunteers. Local emergency services also coordinate volunteer efforts during disasters.

Minnesotans line up to donate money to the Salvation Army's relief efforts for the victims of Hurricane Katrina in September 2005. The money was used to help purchase food, water, and other supplies for people who were left homeless or displaced by the hurricane and its floods.

will they rebuild their lives? If a flood strikes your family's community, government and volunteer agencies will lend a helping hand. Private relief agencies, such as the American Red Cross and the Salvation Army, will provide short-term shelter and assistance to displaced families. The U.S. Army Corps of Engineers will provide drinking water and auxiliary power and will repair bridges. Neighbors and strangers will lend a helping hand.

By following the advice in this book, you and your family will be better prepared for flood, mudslide, and landslide emergencies. Learn about the dangers of floods, mudslides,

American Red Cross volunteers from Pittsburgh, Pennsylvania, distribute care packages to residents whose home was damaged in a New Jersey flood in 2004. Learning about flood preparedness will help you and your family survive flood disasters.

and landslides. Find out about your community's flood emergency plans. If your community doesn't have plans, with the guidance of your parents and teachers, approach community leaders to discuss creating a flood emergency plan. Make a flood emergency plan for your family. Heed flood advisories and evacuate when necessary. Never underestimate the power and effects of floodwaters.

Glossary

debris flow A muddy or liquefied landslide.

dike An earthen barrier that runs alongside a river to protect flood-prone lowlands by confining floodwaters.

El Niño The flow of unusually warm surface waters from the Pacific Ocean toward and along the western coast of South America that disrupts weather patterns worldwide.

flash flood A sudden overflow of water, usually caused by heavy rainfall in a short period.

flash flood warning An advisory issued when flash floods may present a serious threat to life or property.

flash flood watch An advisory issued when a flash flood is likely but not certain to occur within a designated area .

flood The covering of normally dry land by water.

flood control structures Dams, dikes, floodwalls, levees, and other structures built to protect low-lying areas from flooding.

floodplain The portion of a river valley that that has been overflowed by water in the past or could be overflowed by water in the future.

floodwall Reinforced concrete walls built next to a waterway that act as barriers against floodwaters.

flood warning An advisory issued when flooding may present a serious threat to life or property.

flood watch An advisory issued when flooding within a designated watch area is likely to occur but not certain.

global warming An average increase in the earth's temperature, which could cause changes in climate.

hurricane A warm, tropical storm with sustained winds of 64 knots (73.6 mph; 118.5 km/h) or greater.

ice jam A barrier of large, floating chunks of ice that restricts the flow of rivers, causing them to overflow.

landslide The collapse of rocks and soil down a slope.

levee An earthen barrier that runs alongside a river to protect flood-prone lowlands by confining floodwaters.

monsoon A rainy season that occurs the same time each year in certain parts of the world; also, a periodic wind that is specifically found in the Indian Ocean and southern Asia.

mudslide A river of mud that flows down a slope, often carrying rocks, trees, and other debris with it.

National Flood Insurance Program A U.S. government program that provides flood insurance to homeowners and businesses.

NOAA National Oceanic and Atmospheric Administration, a division within the U.S. Department of Commerce, which predicts environmental changes and provides scientific information to governmental officials and the American public.

100-year flood A rare, large flood that happens, on average, once every 100 years.

runoff Water that is not absorbed by soil or vegetation.

storm surge An overflow of water onto coastal areas, caused by hurricane winds.

tsunami A large sea wave created by an earthquake.

watershed An area that drains off into a body of water.

For More Information

American Red Cross
2025 E Street NW
Washington, DC 20006
(202) 303-4498
Disaster Assistance: (866) GET-INFO (866-438-4636)
Donations: (800) HELP-NOW (800-435-7669)
Web site: http://www.redcross.org

Dartmouth Flood Observatory
Department of Geography
Dartmouth College
Hanover, NH 03755
Web site: http://www.dartmouth.edu/~floods

Environmental Protection Agency
Ariel Rios Building
1200 Pennsylvania Avenue NW
Washington, DC 20460
(202) 272-0167
Web site: http://www.epa.gov
For information about cleaning up mold, see http://www.
    epa.gov/iaq/molds/moldguide.html

Federal Emergency Management Agency
500 C Street SW

Washington, DC 20472

(202) 566-1600

Web site: http://www.fema.gov

For restoration tips, see http://www.fema.gov/hazards/
floods/coping.shtm

National Weather Service

1325 East-West Highway

Silver Spring, MD 20910

(301) 713-0224

Web site: http://www.nws.noaa.gov

U.S. Army Corps of Engineers

441 G Street NW

Washington, DC 20314

(202) 761-0011

Web site: http://www.usace.army.mil

For information on how to use sandbags, see
http://www. usace.army.mil/html/offices/op/em/
HowToBag.htm

U.S. Geological Survey

USGS National Center

12201 Sunrise Valley Drive

Reston, VA 20192 USA

(703) 648-4000

Web site: http://www.usgs.gov/

For information on landslides, see http://landslides.usgs.
gov/index.html

Web Sites

Due to the changing nature of Internet links, the Rosen Publishing Group, Inc., has developed an online list of Web sites related to the subject of this book. This site is updated regularly. Please use this link to access the list:

http://www.rosenlinks.com/lep/fffm

For Further Reading

Allaby, Michael. *Floods.* New York, NY: Facts On File, 1998.

Armbruster, Ann. *Floods.* Danbury, CT: Franklin Watts, 1996.

Gallagher, Jim. *The Johnstown Flood.* Broomall, PA: Chelsea House, 2000.

Goodwin, Peter. *Landslides, Slumps, and Creeps.* Danbury, CT: Franklin Watts, 1997.

Harris, Nancy, ed. *Floods.* San Diego, CA: Greenhaven, 2003.

Kline, Lisa Williams. *Floods.* Farmington Hills, MI: Lucent, 2004.

Kurtz, Jane. *River Friendly, River Wild.* New York, NY: Simon & Schuster, 1999.

Lauber, Patricia. *Flood: Wrestling with the Mississippi.* Washington, DC: National Geographic Society, 1996.

Richards, Julie. *Furious Floods.* Broomall, PA: Chelsea House, 2002.

Williams, Mary E., ed. *Hurricanes.* Santa Barbara, CA: Greenhaven, 2004.

Bibliography

Allaby, Michael. *Floods.* New York, NY: Facts On File, 1998.

Allaby, Michael. *Hurricanes.* New York, NY: Facts on File, 1997.

Collier, Michael, and Robert H. Webb. *Floods, Droughts, and Climate Change.* Tucson, AZ: University of Arizona Press, 2002.

Fagan, Brian. *Floods, Famines, and Emperors: El Niño and the Fate of Civilizations.* New York, NY: Basic Books, 1999.

Federal Emergency Management Agency. "Floods." Retrieved February 3, 2005 (http://www.fema.gov/hazards/floods/).

Layton, Peggy. *Emergency Food Storage and Survival Handbook.* Roseville, CA: Prima, 2002.

McCullough, David. *The Johnstown Flood.* New York, NY: Simon and Schuster, 1968.

Miller, E. Willard. *Floods: A Reference Handbook.* Santa Barbara, CA: ABC-CLIO, 2000.

National Weather Service. "Floods, Floods, and Floods: A Preparedness Guide." Retrieved February 5, 2005 (http://www.nws.noaa.gov/om/brochures/ffbro.htm).

PBS NewsHour. "InFocus Floods." Retrieved February 5, 2005 (http://www.pbs.org/newshour/infocus/floods/stories.html).

Reuters. "Flood-Menaced Population to Double by 2050."
June 13, 2004. Retrieved February 2, 2005 (http://www.
reuters.co.uk/newsArticle.jhtml?type=world News&
storyID=528790).

Schnitter, Nicolas J. *A History of Dams.* Brookfield, VT:
Balkema, 1994.

Shallat, Tom A. *Structures in the Stream: Water, Science, and
the Rise of the U.S. Army Corps of Engineers.* Austin, TX:
University of Texas Press, 1994.

Smith, Keith, and Roy Ward. *Floods: Physical Processes and
Human Impacts.* New York, NY: Wiley, 1998.

Index

About the Author

G. S. Prentzas, who graduated with honors from the University of North Carolina School of Law, is a writer and editor living in New York. He developed a keen interest in floods at age ten, when floodwaters submerged his aunt's house in North Carolina. Mr. Prentzas has written more than a dozen books for young readers.

Photo Credits

Cover, pp.1, 5, 8, 11, 12, 13, 18, 19, 20, 28, 29, 37, 40, 41, 42, 50, 52, 53 © AP/Wide World Photos; p. 16 by Tahara Anderson; p. 25 courtesy of the US Army Corps of Engineers; p. 34 http://www.crh.noaa.gov/fgf; p. 39 © Alan Schein Photography/Corbis; p. 45 © Andrew Holbrooke/Corbis; p. 47 © Fritz Hoffman/The Image Works.

Designer: Tahara Anderson; Editor: Kathy Kuhtz Campbell